For Joseph Goodhart,
with love

First published in 2005 in Great Britain by
Barrington Stoke Ltd, 18 Walker Street, Edinburgh EH3 7LP
www.barringtonstoke.co.uk
Reprinted 2007

ISBN 978-1-84299-290-6

Printed in Great Britain by Bell & Bain Ltd

Barrington Stoke gratefully acknowledges support from the
Scottish Arts Council towards the publication of the
fyi series

Scottish
Arts Council
LOTTERY FUNDED

Contents

1   Hot Air   1

2   It's Not Fair!   6

3   Thinking   10

4   Bricks and Sticks   17

5   And Straw   24

6   Huff and Puff   33

7   The Best   41

8   And the Winner Is ...   49

    Connor's Eco Notebook   57

    Author and Illustrator Fact Files   62

Chapter 1
Hot Air

"Get off!" said Connor. "I'm reading a book!"

"Shift over," said Adam. "I need some room on the table for my model."

"Will you two shut up!" shouted Ben. "I can't hear the telly!"

"It's a great book, this," said Connor.

"What's it about?" asked Adam.

"The environment," said Connor.

"Boring," said Adam.

"Put a sock in it!" said Ben.

"Did you know that there are gases all around the world?" Connor went on.

"'Course I did, or there'd be nothing to breathe," said Adam.

"Yes, but I bet you didn't know that the gases keep the Earth warm," said Connor. "It says here that the gases let some of the heat from the sun through to warm the Earth. Then they hold the heat around the Earth so that the Earth stays a bit warm even when it's night-time and the sun isn't shining on it. Like a greenhouse letting in sunshine and keeping plants warm. That's why ..."

"Shut up!" Ben threw a cushion at Connor.

"Yeah, take that book away and read it to yourself," said Adam.

So that's what Connor did. He went over to his bed where he lay with his fingers in his ears, and went on reading.

More and more people on Earth are burning more and more fuel, so the layer of greenhouse gases is getting thicker. Because it's thicker, it's keeping more heat close to the Earth. So the Earth is getting hotter. This is called "Global Warming".

If there were no greenhouse gases, the Earth would become so cold at night, and in winter, that the sea would freeze. Many of the world's animals and plants would die out.

Greenhouse gases include –

carbon dioxide from cars and lorries, power plants and factories.

methane created by the production of different fuels, by farm animals, and by rotting rubbish.

nitrous oxide created by farming and by the burning of fuels.

CFCs coming from old fridges, spray cans and some factories.

Chapter 2
It's Not Fair!

"Blimey," said Connor and he put down the book for a moment. "Did you know that we're making the world hotter?"

"Wicked!" said Adam. "I like it hot."

"Shut UP, you two!" said Ben, and he turned up the volume on the telly.

Connor just shouted louder, "No, it isn't good that the world's getting hotter. It's

6

melting ice at the South Pole and the North Pole and that's making more sea. More sea means higher tides and floods. These floods are reaching places where people live, drowning them and washing away their homes and farms and everything they own."

"I wish someone would drown you!" said Ben. "Can't you see, I'm trying to watch telly!"

"But this is important ..." shouted Connor.

"JUST SHUT UP!" yelled Ben. He swung his arm to thump Connor. Connor ducked. Ben's arm hit Adam's model.

"Look what you've done! It's a mess!"

"I never ..." began Ben.

"Get off!" shouted Adam.

Crash! Bang! Tear! Crunch!

"STOP!" shouted Mrs Hogg from the doorway. "Just look at the mess you've made! What's the matter with you lot?"

So they all told her, all at once.

"He started ..."

"I only ..."

"They were ..."

It ended together with all three brothers shouting, "IT'S NOT FAIR that we have to share such a tiny room!"

Mrs Hogg looked at the little bedroom. She looked at the size of her three sons. She looked at their faces. "You're right," she said. "There isn't enough room for you all in here. But I don't know what we can do about it."

Chapter 3
Thinking

At dinner, Mrs Hogg looked round the table. "Your dad's had an idea," she said. "Tell them, Wolfgang." Mr Hogg had had an idea about the bedrooms.

"I've been looking at the costs, and I've worked out that we could build an extra room onto this house. But we can only afford to make one small new bedroom, so two of you will still have to share the old one."

"So who gets the new bedroom?" asked Adam. "I'm the oldest. It should be mine."

"Why?" said Connor. "I've never had a room to myself!"

"Nor have I," said Ben. "It's not fair if ..."

"Will you all shut up and listen?" said Mr Hogg. "I'll make this as fair as I can. We will have a competition. The winner of that competition will get the new room."

"What sort of competition?" asked Adam.

"Ah," said Mr Hogg, "I've been thinking. It will be a competition to find out which of you boys is going to be the most helpful building the extra room. It's only fair that the one who helps the most gets to have the room."

"But …?" said Connor.

"How …?" said Adam.

"Why …?" said Ben.

Mr Hogg lifted up a hand to shut them up. "The competition is to build a shelter in the wood behind the house. You've got the weekend to make your shelter, and then your mum and I will come and judge which of them is the best. The boy who builds the best one wins."

"And the winner gets the new room?" said Ben.

"That's the idea," said Mr Hogg. "So, you'd better get on with it, hadn't you?"

Adam and Ben ran off, both fighting to get to the wood first as they raced to find the best place to build a shelter.

But Connor didn't move.

"What are you doing, just standing there, boy?" asked Mr Hogg. "Go and start building with the others!"

"I'm thinking," said Connor.

"Thinking?" said Mr Hogg. "What's the use of thinking when there's work to be done?"

Connor was thinking about the competition. And he was thinking about what he had read in his book. He asked his dad, "Did you know that there are almost six and a half billion people in the world?"

"What's that got to do with building a shelter?" said Mr Hogg.

"Well, there are all those billions of people. And there are more being added all the time. Even if you take away the people dying as well as adding the ones being born, there are two more people being added to the population of the world every second."

"But what's that got to do with ...?"

"The extra people have all got to live somewhere, haven't they? Some of them live in houses, like we do. But lots of them live in tiny shelters made of boxes or plastic or twigs or just anything else they can find."

"Did you get all that out of your book?" asked Mr Hogg.

"And from the telly," said Connor. "And it's not fair, because the rich people are making all this stuff to build houses. Then they have to transport it to the building sites in lorries. And heating big buildings makes lots more greenhouse gases."

"Oh, I see," said Mr Hogg.

"So," said Connor, "global warming is mostly the rich people's fault. But when the Earth heats up it's the poor people who get flooded and starved."

Mr Hogg looked puzzled. "But what's that got to do with making a shelter in the woods? Get on with it, boy! Follow your brothers and get started or you won't have a hope of winning the competition!"

Chapter 4
Bricks and Sticks

So Connor went into the wood and found Adam in a wide gap between the trees.

"What are you doing, spying on me?" said Adam. "You can't make your shelter here. This is my place. See? I've marked my bit of land."

That's what animals do, thought Connor. *They mark out their own patch.*

"Get lost," said Adam. "I've got a phone call to make and I don't want you to hear what I'm saying."

Connor knew what Adam was doing. Adam was the one who liked to help Dad after school and in the holidays. He knew quite a lot about building. Connor had seen Adam looking up at the sign over Dad's builder's yard. The sign said, Wolfgang Hogg, Builders. Connor knew that Adam dreamed that sign might one day say ...

and that Adam would be the son on the sign. *Adam's really going to try to impress Dad*, thought Connor. *He's going to make his house of bricks. I'd be no good at doing that.*

As Connor went off to find Ben, he could hear Adam on his mobile phone.

"Is that the builders' merchant?" said Adam. "I'd like to order some bricks and cement to be delivered. Put them on my dad's account please. That's Wolfgang Hogg. I need a wheelbarrow and a bucket too. I need it all now."

Ben was deeper into the wood, with trees all round him.

"Hi!" said Connor.

"Go and find your own place," said Ben. But Connor stopped to watch Ben for a while.

"What are you doing?" asked Connor.

"I'm not telling you," said Ben, but then he did tell. "It was on that telly programme last night," he said. "They were using wooden poles and sticks to make shelters." Ben drew on the earth with a twig. "You can make a round shelter like an American tepee.

"But long poles are hard to get. So I'm doing a tent shape like this.

"It won't take long. I bet I'm finished before you."

"There's a long pole there," said Connor.

"That'll do for the pole along the top," said Ben. "Thanks!" He lifted the pole and put it between the branches of two trees. "Perfect fit! I've only got the walls to do now, then I'm done."

I'd better get started on my shelter,
thought Connor, *or Ben will be finished
before I've even begun.* Connor went off
frowning. He was thinking so hard that he
didn't look where he was going and – crash!
"Blimey!" – one foot went down a rabbit
hole and Connor fell, splat, onto the muddy
ground. Connor sat and rubbed his ankle.
"Flipping rabbits!" he said. But then the
frown cleared from his face. *A hole in the
ground*, he thought. *A hole in the ground*

can be a good place to live. He remembered
a book he'd read about wild animals in
America –

*Muskrats are wise home builders. They dig
holes into the ground and the Earth protects them
from extremes of heat or cold. Some animal
instinct for weather tells the muskrats how
severe the winter is going to be. So, if in the
autumn you see muskrats digging holes that are
deeper than usual, you can be sure that we are
going to have a very cold winter indeed. The cold
won't bother the muskrats. They will be snug,
deep in their earth holes.*

I wonder? thought Connor.

Chapter 5
And Straw

"How are the shelters coming along?" asked Mr Hogg over the supper table.

"I've only done the concrete floor so far," said Adam. "But my shelter is going to be really strong when it's finished."

"Mine's almost finished already," said Ben.

"And what about yours, Connor?" asked Mrs Hogg. "How's it going?"

"OK," said Connor, but his brothers laughed.

"He hasn't even started!"

"What on earth have you been doing all day then, Connor?" asked Mr Hogg.

"Planning," said Connor. "Reading and finding out what will work best."

"Just like you!" said Adam. "You can't make a book into a shelter, you know, not unless it's a shelter for a mouse!"

"You've only got tomorrow left to do the whole thing," said Ben.

"No problem," said Connor.

"Let's hope that the weather stays fine," said Mrs Hogg. "I'll give you each some money for fish and chips from the village, then you can stay out all day."

They were up early next morning. Adam wanted to get started on his walls. He needed to mix more mortar and lay the bricks properly, one by one. Ben's shelter was complete, but he went looking for interesting leaves and bits of wood and pebbles to decorate it with. And Connor? Connor stood and looked up at the sky. He pointed a finger and frowned.

"You look crazy," said Ben. "What are you doing?"

"Seeing where the sun is."

"Why?"

"So that I can choose a place for my shelter that faces the sun," said Connor.

"You're thick!" said Ben. "What sort of shelter is that going to be?"

"A kind of cave," said Connor. "Facing the sun to get warmth and light, and with snug walls to keep out the wind."

Ben spun a finger around close to his head to show what he thought of Connor. But Connor found what he was looking for – a tall earth bank with a dip into it like a shallow cave. *But I'm not going to dig deeper to make a proper cave*, Connor thought to himself. *That would take too long and make a place that was too dark. I'm going to build forwards and use this just as the back of my shelter.*

"Can I borrow your wheelbarrow?" Connor asked Adam.

"Where are you going with it?"

"To the farm," said Connor.

"The farm! You're stupid, you are," said Adam.

Connor pushed the barrow down the lane to the farm. He promised to sweep the farmer's yard the next weekend and paid his fish and chip lunch money in return for some bales of straw and a lift back to the wood.

Connor piled the bales on top of each other to build a curved wall in front of his cave. He made it curved because that is the shape that all animals and birds use for nests and burrows. A circle is the shape

that gives you the biggest area inside for the least wall. It's the walls that use up building materials and walls that let heat in and out. Connor left two gaps in his wall, one for a door and one for a window. The straw bales were heavy to lift, but Connor managed to pile them one on top of another. It took less than an hour to build his wall. Then Connor put sticks between the straw wall and the top of the cave. That was the frame for his roof.

"Can I borrow your spade?" Connor asked Adam.

"Haven't you got any tools of your own?" said Adam angrily as he built up his shelter, small brick by small brick. "Yeah, you can take the spade."

Connor dug up blocks of grassy earth. As dark clouds filled the sky, Connor put the chunks of earth onto his roof frame. He thought of the Vikings who had made grassy roofs for their homes over a thousand years ago. He thought of the families in America who made homes on the empty prairies over a hundred years ago. They used chunks of grassy earth to make whole houses sometimes, because there weren't any trees on the prairies. Buying and moving planks cost a lot of money, and wooden homes and stables weren't warm. Connor's earth roof didn't take long to finish.

The sky got dark. Rain began to fall.

"Oh, no!" said Adam, putting up his hood. He slapped mortar onto bricks and kept building upwards as fast as he could.

"No problem!" said Ben when he felt the rain. He just crept inside his stick tent shelter. He lay there and dozed off. But soon he was muttering, "Hey! What? Oh, heck!" Rain ran down the twigs and dripped onto him. Ben shivered.

Rain? Just what I need, thought Connor. He picked up the spade and mixed the soil in his earthy hole into mud. Then he slapped the mud onto the wet straw walls.

Chapter 6
Huff and Puff

The rain had turned to hail by the time Mr and Mrs Hogg set out to judge the shelters.

"This weather will be a good test of whatever those boys have built," said Mr Hogg.

"I'm sure they've all made lovely shelters," said Mrs Hogg. The wind was so

strong that it blew Mrs Hogg's umbrella inside out. "Oops!" she added as she bumped into Mr Hogg who had stopped suddenly. Mr Hogg slowly lifted an arm and pointed.

"WHAT," he said, "is THAT?"

"I think it must be Adam's shelter, dear," said Mrs Hogg.

"But it's built with bricks!"

"That's right, Dad," said Adam and grinned. "See? I'm building a proper home."

"Where did those bricks come from?"

"Um, I ordered them," said Adam. "Er, on your account, Dad. I thought you wouldn't mind."

"WHAT? And there's my best spade that I've been looking for everywhere! And a bag of cement left open to the rain. It'll go solid in no time. ADAM!"

"Oh, stop it!" said Mrs Hogg. "Don't huff and puff so. Adam's made a lovely bit of wall."

"It's not quite finished," said Adam. "I haven't had time to do the roof yet."

They stepped through the gap where the door should have been and stood inside. They shivered, getting wetter and wetter as they looked at the low brick wall which only came up to their knees.

"The wall does stop the wind a little," said Mrs Hogg. "But it's a bit chilly in here, Adam. A bit wet. Not very cosy."

"But if I had more time ..."

"... you would have cost me even more and wasted more good building materials," said Mr Hogg. "Have you any idea how much that lot cost?"

"Now then, Wolfgang," said Mrs Hogg. "Let's go and see what the other boys have done."

Ben was busy poking bits of twig into his house of sticks.

"I thought you said you'd finished yours ages ago," said Adam.

"I did," said Ben. "Only bits keep blowing off because of the wind."

Adam laughed. "At least bricks don't blow away!"

"At least sticks are free and make a shelter that's finished on time," said Ben. "I get extra marks for being finished on time, don't I, Dad?"

"Can we go inside, dear?" asked Mrs Hogg, who was getting very, very wet.

"If you don't mind going on your hands and knees," said Ben.

It was a tight fit for them all inside. They had to bend their heads and huddle up close. Cold drips ran down their necks.

"Quite noisy in here, isn't it?" said Mrs Hogg. The wind huffed and puffed and they could hear trees bending and cracking. The gaps in the stick walls let in the rain and cold. "This must be how it feels to be a bird in a nest," said Mrs Hogg.

"Except that birds make their nests so that they don't fall to bits in the first puff of wind," said Mr Hogg. "This shelter's not going to last for a day." He was shaking his head. "Let's get this over with, shall we?

What's Connor got to show us? Anything at all?"

Adam looked at Ben and they both sniggered. "I think that Connor's made his house out of straw," said Adam.

"Straw and mud!" said Ben.

"Flipping heck, it gets worse and worse," said Mr Hogg. "Still, I suppose we'd better go and see."

The stick house fell to pieces behind them.

40

Chapter 7
The Best

"Come in," said Connor. "Plenty of room for everyone!"

They stepped into Connor's shelter.

"Ooh, I say!" said Mrs Hogg. "Somewhere to sit! And it's dry and quiet and out of the wind. It's light too. Very nice, Connor love."

"Yeah," said Adam. "But my shelter is stronger, being made of bricks. This won't last much longer than Ben's stick shelter did."

"It will," said Connor. "There are straw houses with people living in them that were built hundreds of years ago. There's one that's over 700 years old."

"700 year-old straw bales?" asked Ben.

"No, not bales," said Connor. "It was only after they got steam machines on the farms that they had the straw in bales. That began in the 1840s. Before that the straw was mixed with mud and stuck to a wooden

frame. They called the mix of mud and straw cob. Cob sets so hard it can last almost forever. But now we have bales it's much easier. You use straw bales like big bricks."

"But why would anyone want to use straw?" said Adam.

"Because ..." began Connor.

"Here we go!" said Ben.

"No, listen to him, you two. This is interesting," said Mrs Hogg. "Go on, Connor love."

"Well, building with straw is a lot cheaper than using bricks, for a start."

"Hear that, Adam?" said Mr Hogg.

"Straw bales don't cost much. It would take about 400 bales like this to make a

house with three bedrooms. That'd cost under £1,000. Bricks for the same size house would cost over £10,000!"

"Now, that's a big saving!" said Mr Hogg.

"And of course you don't have to pay for straw bales to be carried a long way like bricks are. Wheat is grown all over the place. Straw is what's left over after they've taken off the corn to make flour or animal food."

"But straw gets used as bedding for horses and cows, doesn't it?" said Ben.

"Only some of it," said Connor. "There's about four million tonnes of straw left over in this country every year. That's enough to make 450,000 houses every year! If they did that, then there wouldn't be nearly so many bricks and so much concrete made as there is now. It's making building materials and carrying them about the place that makes a lot of the greenhouse gases in this country."

"Not those gases again!" said Ben.

"Shush," said Mrs Hogg. "I hear what you're saying, Connor. Go on."

"Well, it's even better than that," said Connor. He was waving his arms about. "You see, when you grow the wheat, the plants take in the bad carbon dioxide from the air and turn it into oxygen which is good for us."

"The straw does make a nice, warm, dry house," said Mrs Hogg, as she took off her coat.

"Dry and warm because it's well insulated," said Connor. "It costs 75% less to heat a straw house than it does to heat a normal house. And that means far fewer greenhouse gases getting into the air."

"But straw looks ugly," said Ben. "Not like my stick house with flowers in it and everything."

"A straw house can be as fancy as you like!" said Connor. "You cover the straw with a sort of plaster and paint it however you want. You could do whatever you like with the earth roof. You could grow flowers on it. Or perhaps even herbs to pick for cooking or to smell nice. You could give it a different haircut every week, if you wanted!"

Mr Hogg counted off on his fingers. "So a straw house is good for the environment. It's cheap to build and to run. It can last a very long time and it can look nice. It insulates for heat and cold, and sound too. Anything else?"

"Yep," said Connor. "You don't have to bother so much with builders. You can make your own straw house because it's so easy and quick. Ooops, sorry, Dad!"

Adam grinned. "Ha ha! You won't win now, Connor. Not after putting Dad out of work!"

They all looked at Mr Hogg, wondering if he would start huffing and puffing, but he didn't. He smiled.

"I've made up my mind," he said, and folded his arms. "The winner of this competition is ...

Chapter 8
And the Winner Is ...

"... all three of you!" said Mr Hogg. "You've all won."

"How can ...?"

"But that's not ...!"

"It is fair," said Mr Hogg. "Because you boys are going to get a bedroom each. If Connor is right about building with straw, then we can afford to build on two new rooms."

So that's what they did. Connor worked out the plans. Mr Hogg and Adam did most of the building. Ben made the new rooms look nice.

"But who's going to have the old room?" asked Adam.

"Not me," said Connor. "Building with straw was my idea."

"Well, I made the new rooms look the way they do!" said Ben.

"I did most of the building work!" said Adam.

"It's not fair if ..."

And they began to fight. Crash. Punch. Hit. Shout.

"Here we go again!" said Mrs Hogg. She looked at Mr Hogg. "Perhaps you and I could make a little straw house for ourselves. They do keep the noise out so well."

And a few years later that's just what they did. When Mr Hogg stopped work, the three sons made their mum and dad the best and most peaceful little house to live in for the rest of their lives.

HOME SWEET ECO-FRIENDLY HOME

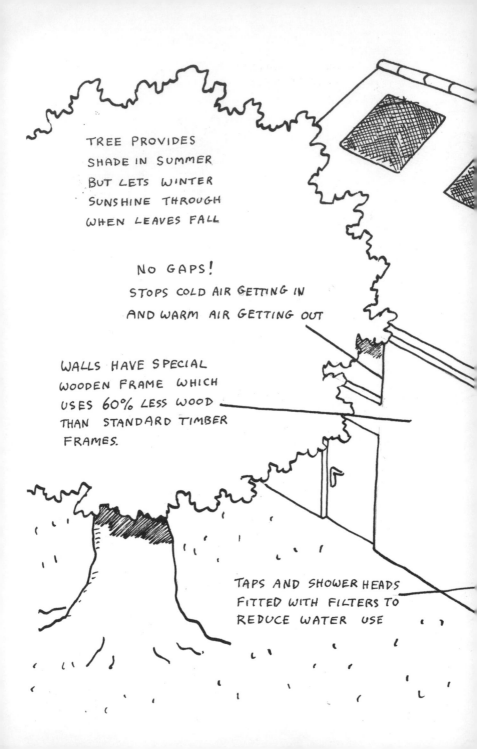

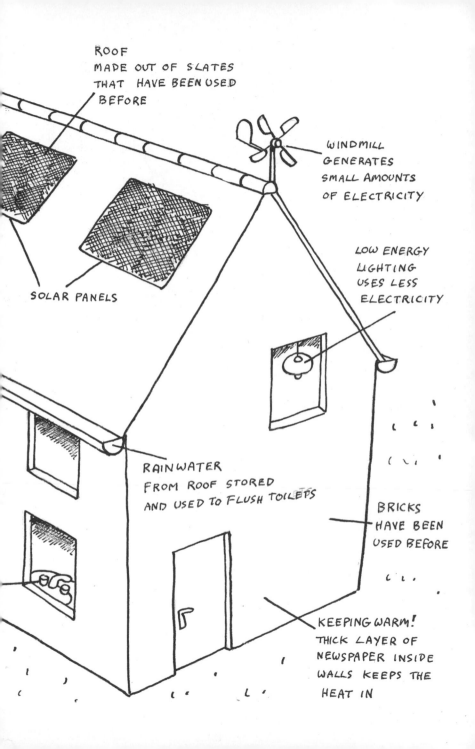

ROOF
MADE OUT OF SLATES
THAT HAVE BEEN USED
BEFORE

WINDMILL
GENERATES
SMALL AMOUNTS
OF ELECTRICITY

LOW ENERGY
LIGHTING
USES LESS
ELECTRICITY

SOLAR PANELS

RAINWATER
FROM ROOF STORED
AND USED TO FLUSH TOILETS

BRICKS
HAVE BEEN
USED BEFORE

KEEPING WARM!
THICK LAYER OF
NEWSPAPER INSIDE
WALLS KEEPS THE
HEAT IN

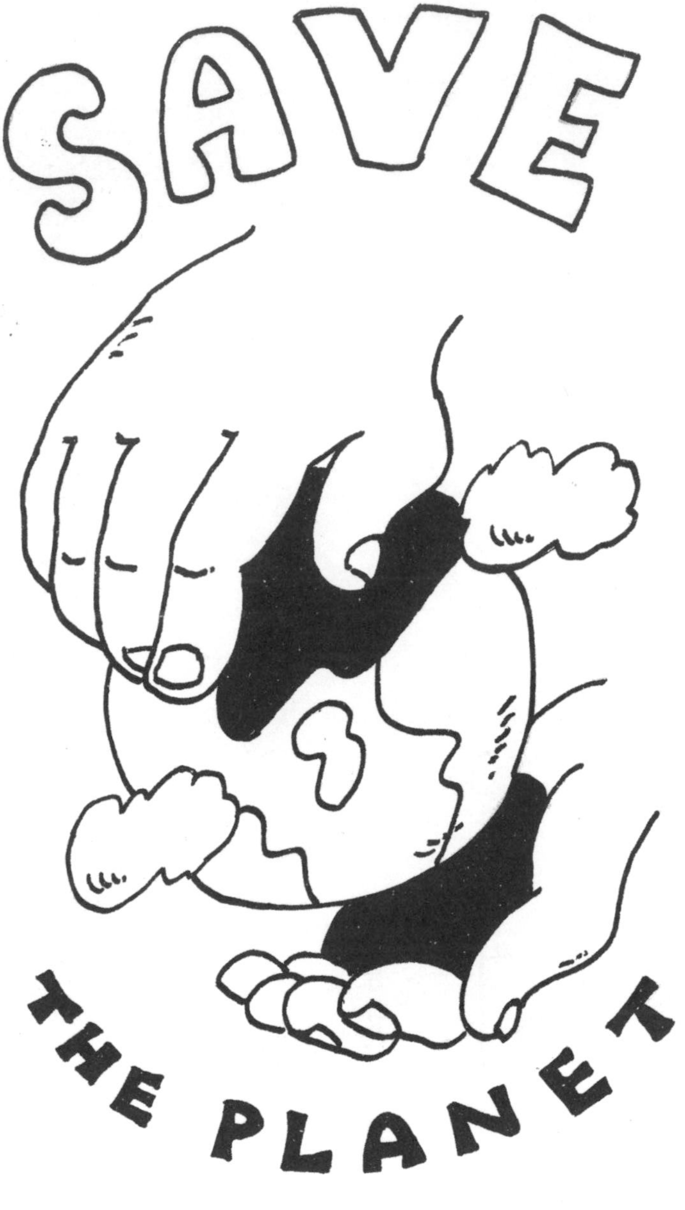
SAVE
THE PLANET

The Earth is getting hotter!

As the Earth gets warmer, the ice at the South and North Poles is melting. The melted ice water is making sea levels higher. Higher sea levels cause flooding where there hasn't been flooding before. Thousands of people's homes and crops are being destroyed by massive floods.

It's poor people who suffer the most from global warming

There are almost six and a half billion people in the world. The number of people goes up by two every second because there are more people being born than there are dying. Where do these people all live? The lucky ones live in rich houses. Lots more people live in poor shelters. Some people have nowhere to live at all.

Making and moving materials to build houses for the rich people creates greenhouse gases that are making the world warmer. But it is mostly poor homes that are in the places that flood from the rising sea levels.

How we used to build houses

Nearly two thousand years ago, the Viking people living in Norway used turf to make roofs for their houses and stables.

People around the world still use mud and turf as a building material. Over a hundred years ago, pioneer families in America made turf homes on the prairies because there were few trees. They made houses and stables using turf to fill in a timber frame. It was cheaper than buying

WOOD FRAME   TURF

AMERICAN PIONEER

and hauling planks from far away. And it made cosier homes because turf insulates better than planks of wood.

How should Adam and Ben have built their houses?

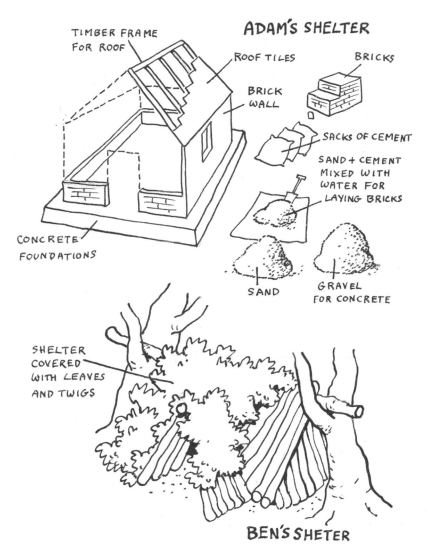

ADAM'S SHELTER

TIMBER FRAME
FOR ROOF

ROOF TILES

BRICKS

BRICK
WALL

SACKS OF CEMENT

SAND + CEMENT
MIXED WITH
WATER FOR
LAYING BRICKS

CONCRETE
FOUNDATIONS

SAND

GRAVEL
FOR CONCRETE

SHELTER
COVERED
WITH LEAVES
AND TWIGS

BEN'S SHETER

AUTHOR FACT FILE
PIPPA GOODHART

Do you recycle your bottles and newspapers?
Yes, and put peelings into the compost.

Do you re-use old envelopes?
**Yes, I put sticky labels over the old
address.**

*Do you turn off the light when the room is
empty?*
**Yes, and I nag the rest of the family to do
the same.**

*Do you put on a jumper instead of turning up
the heating?*
**Yes. I wear two fleeces and a jumper
sometimes when I'm in the house on my
own!**

ILLUSTRATOR FACT FILE
MARTIN REMPHRY

Do you recycle your bottles and newspapers?
Yes.

Do you re-use old envelopes?
Yes, especially to send my illustrations to the publishers.

Do you turn off the light when the room is empty?
Yes, but I often forget.

Do you put on a jumper instead of turning up the heating?
Both! We are renovating our new house and some of the walls and ceilings are missing so it is very draughty.

Barrington Stoke would like to thank all its readers for commenting on the manuscript before publication and in particular:

Aroosa Ahmed
Mohammed Ammer
Ibra Arshad
Amar Ayuh
Aamina Bibi
Efra Bibi Yusuf
Jannat Bi Saleem
Dilshad Bundhoo
Shirley Davids
Jacqueline Ann Daniel
Sam Evans
Kiran Faraz
Craig Fathers
Javairia Fatima
Kiran Fiaz
Matthew Gilbert
Jane Griffiths
Ameer Hamzah
Shakina Hayat
Chris Heeley
Amjid Hussain
Awaiz Hussain
Iram Hussain
Memoona Hussain
Tasnimul Islam
Ismah Jabeen Javed
Samara Jaivaid
Hannah Eleanor Jones
Diane Killock
Faisal Zakar Khan

Afifa Madni
Urmah Majid
Usma Malik
Sarina Mariah Saib
Farah Naaz
Shabeena Niwaz
Charlotte Pearson
Sali Putt
Clare Raftery
Aminah Rehman
Muhammed Shabaz Pervez
Sameera Sultan
Charlotte Taylor
Emma Taylor
Mrs Rachel Taylor
Aram Ul Nisa
Muhammed Yhaya Ahmed
Adeel Zafar
Mohammed Zafran

Become a Consultant!

Would you like to give us feedback on our titles before they are published? Contact us at the email address below – we'd love to hear from you!

info@barringtonstoke.co.uk   www.barringtonstoke.co.uk